PENELOPE
CHRISTMAS REUNION

SHARON E. McKAY

**Look for the other Penelope stories
in Our Canadian Girl**

PENELOPE
CHRISTMAS REUNION
SHARON E. McKAY

PENGUIN
CANADA

PENGUIN CANADA

Published by the Penguin Group

Penguin Group (Canada), 10 Alcorn Avenue, Toronto, Ontario, Canada M4V 3B2
(a division of Pearson Penguin Canada Inc.)

Penguin Group (USA) Inc., 375 Hudson Street, New York, New York 10014, U.S.A.
Penguin Books Ltd, 80 Strand, London WC2R 0RL, England
Penguin Ireland, 25 St Stephen's Green, Dublin 2, Ireland (a division of Penguin Books Ltd)
Penguin Group (Australia), 250 Camberwell Road, Camberwell, Victoria 3124, Australia
(a division of Pearson Australia Group Pty Ltd)
Penguin Books India Pvt Ltd, 11 Community Centre, Panchsheel Park, New Delhi – 110 017, India
Penguin Group (NZ), Cnr Airborne and Rosedale Roads, Albany, Auckland, New Zealand
(a division of Pearson New Zealand Ltd)
Penguin Books (South Africa) (Pty) Ltd, 24 Sturdee Avenue, Rosebank, Johannesburg 2196,
South Africa

Penguin Books Ltd, Registered Offices: 80 Strand, London WC2R 0RL, England

First published 2004

1 2 3 4 5 6 7 8 9 10   (WEB)

Copyright © Sharon E. McKay, 2004
Cover illustration © Ron Lightburn, 2004
Chapter-opener and interior illustrations © Janet Wilson, 2004
Design: Matthews Communications Design Inc.
Map © Sharon Matthews

Publisher's note: This book is a work of fiction. Names, characters, places, and incidents either
are the product of the author's imagination or are used fictitiously, and any resemblance
to actual persons living or dead, events, or locales is entirely coincidental.

Manufactured in Canada.

LIBRARY AND ARCHIVES CANADA CATALOGUING IN PUBLICATION

McKay, Sharon E.
Penelope : Christmas reunion / Sharon E. McKay.

(Our Canadian girl)
"Penelope, book four".
ISBN 0-14-301670-9

I. Title. II. Title: Christmas reunion. III. Series.

PS8575.K2898P455   2004   jC813'.6   C2004-903061-2

Visit the Penguin Group (Canada) website at **www.penguin.ca**

Another one!

Who would have thought that I could get so lucky!

To my beautiful niece Kendra

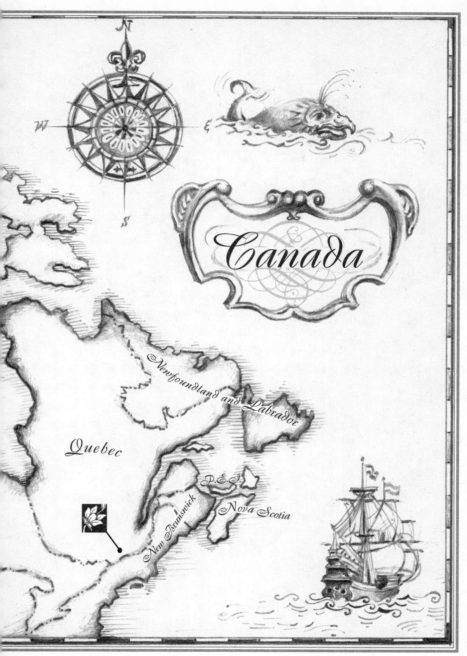

Canada

Quebec

Newfoundland and Labrador

P.E.I.

New Brunswick

Nova Scotia

 Marks the location of the story

PENELOPE'S STORY CONCLUDES

THE WAR THAT BEGAN to great fanfare on August 4, 1914, ended after much regret on November 11, 1918. The Christmas of 1918 was an emotional time for all Canadians as they dealt with the consequences of a war that had devastated the world.

The population of Canada was only 8 million, and an estimated 60,000 Canadian lives were lost in the war. A further 229,000 men were wounded. More than 600,000 men served in the Canadian army, and another 21,000 Canadians went into the British Flying services.

By the end of the war, the Canadian economy was in terrible shape, and there were food shortages. The *temporary income tax* introduced in 1917 remains in place today. Further, French Canadians had deeply resented conscription (military draft) forced on them by Prime Minister Borden in 1917. Riots occurred and many French people began to openly speak of *separation* from Canada. Today that dreadful word still threatens to divide our country.

Penny's family, like most, adapted to the changes forced on them by the war. Penny was now well established in Montreal at Miss Potter's School for Girls. The Christmas of 1918 held special meaning for Penny. Papa, Emily, and Maggie would be coming to Montreal. Her family would be together again.

Montreal, December 21, 1918

"Wake up!" Penny's teeth chattered. The furnace was acting up again, and it was cold in Sally's bedroom. "Sally!" Penny's whisper turned into a hiss as she hopped about on the round rag rug beside Sally's bed.

Sally's bedroom was a lovely little room with pristine white curtains, rosy pink walls, a soft plum-coloured chair, and a pink-and-green bowl and jug on top of a washstand.

The room was at the very top of the house. Sally was the only maid to live above stairs. Nancy, the daily, lived in Griffintown and took the streetcar back and forth every day. Cook's bedroom was off the kitchen. Duncan and old Arthur, the chauffeur, lived in the carriage house behind the main house.

"Sally, are you awake?" Penny gave her a gentle poke. She was getting colder by the minute.

"What time is it?" Sally didn't even open her eyes.

"It's morning!" Penny's teeth were now clicking together so fast they were nearly playing a tune. Sally reached for her clock. "It's five o'clock! I don't have to get up for a whole hour yet!" She moaned, banged her pillow with her fist, and rolled over.

A warm gap in the bedcovers was left behind. The iron bedstead squeaked terribly as Penny slid in beside Sally. "Aren't you excited?" Penny whispered. The war was over, Papa and Maggie and Emily would arrive in a few hours, and—not that this was as important as everything else—Penny was pretty sure that she had passed all her Christmas exams at Miss Potter's School for Girls. This would be the best Christmas ever.

There was one fly in the ointment. (That was one of Cook's expressions.) Aunt Colleen's brother, Robert, had disappeared. He had written from France on November 12, the day after peace was declared, saying that he would be on the first ship home. They had not heard from him since. Grandma seemed especially concerned. If Aunt Colleen was like a daughter to Grandma, then Uncle Robert was like a son.

"I wish I could go to Windsor Station with Arthur to meet them. Sally, are you still sleeping?" asked Penny as she peered over Sally's shoulder. Sally answered by groaning again.

Penny flopped onto half the pillow. Just *thinking* about the day ahead made her giggle. Papa would arrive in Montreal on the 1:45 train from Halifax. Aunt Colleen had gone to Toronto two days ago to collect Emily and Maggie. They would arrive at the same station fifteen minutes later. Seven people could ride in Grandma's brand new Cadillac, but Grandma had said that with three grown-ups (including Arthur) two children, and the luggage, there would be no room for either of them. Penny had pleaded with Grandma and even offered to walk home, but Grandma was adamant. Penny would wait at the house. It was the practical and proper thing to do. Stuff and nonsense all those public displays of affection at train stations, Grandma had said.

Penny pulled up the blankets. The radiator was awfully quiet. It was usually hissing and knocking as if a small animal were caught inside.

"Do you think that Maggie and Emily will like their room?" asked Penny. This time Sally didn't even groan.

Duncan and Penny had dragged boxes of Mama's old toys down from the attic. Sally had helped paint the dollhouse, and Duncan had made a new saddle for the rocking horse. Grandma had said that Maggie and Emily could have all of Mama's toys, except for Martha, Mama's doll. Martha belonged to Penny. Penny started humming *Joy to the World*.

Everyone had been working hard to get the house ready for Christmas. They had decorated inside with green cedar boughs and great golden globes that Sally said had come all the way from Italy. And at this very moment, a large Christmas tree was propped against the carriage house. Penny didn't know the third verse to *Joy to the World* so she switched to *Away in a Manger*.

With a deep sigh, Sally turned over and stared wide-eyed at the ceiling.

"Finally! You are awake," said Penny.

"I don't suppose I'll be getting back to sleep now." Sally picked up the clock. "Five thirty. Well at least Duncan will have the kitchen fire going by now." The radiator suddenly rumbled as if to announce that it was working again. Most likely Duncan was in the basement tinkering with it. Duncan was brilliant at fixing things, although he was about to give up on what he called *the monster in the basement*. Sally rolled out of bed and slipped her feet into her waiting slippers.

"Sally, do you know how to make boxty?" Penny kneeled on the bed.

"I do indeed. *'Boxty on the griddle, boxty on the pan, if you don't eat boxty, you'll never get a man.'*" Sally sang while giving her hair a stiff brushing.

"Papa used to sing that too. It made Mama laugh. Could we make some for my father? Oh, please?"

"Well, we do have leftover mashed potatoes, that I know. But sure Cook will get her knickers in a twist if we use her ovens." Sally turned her back to Penny, yanked a thick flannel chest protector over her head, and then quickly laced her corset over top.

"Could we make it before she wakes up?"

Sally pulled a slip over her head, then turned and looked into Penny's pleading eyes. "Sure, what's the harm?"

"Oh, thank you!" The bed squeaked fiercely as Penny bounced off it.

Penny fidgeted as Sally poured cold water from the jug into her wash bowl and washed her face. A spray of brown freckles across her nose stood out against her pale skin. Penny watched Sally peer into the spotty mirror above the washstand. "It's a terrible thing to be saddled with a pug nose," Sally sighed as she patted her face dry. Sally was always talking about her freckles and nose, but Penny thought Sally was quite pretty. Sally stepped into her maid's uniform, buttoned up the front, and then tied an apron around her waist.

"Let me do your hair." Sally held up her hairbrush and nodded her head towards the dressing table. Penny sat down and looked into the mirror. For the millionth time, she wished that she had inherited Mama's blond hair, like Emily and Maggie had. When the sun was shining on Penny's red hair, it looked as if her head were on fire.

Sally expertly plaited Penny's hair into one thick braid. "Get dressed and meet me in the kitchen in ten minutes," she said as she shooed Penny out the door.

It didn't take Penny ten minutes to dress—it barely took her five. She was breathless as she bolted down the servants' stairs and ran into the basement kitchen.

"What's this then? Has the young lady of the house come to make tea for the servants?" Duncan grinned. He tossed a shovel full of coal into the oven with one hand, while he scratched a match to light the top of the stove with the other.

"Help yourself to your own tea," snapped Sally as she came out of the larder carrying a bowl of leftover mashed potatoes. Sally was sweet on Duncan and he was in love with her, but neither one would admit it. Of course, they were too young to marry, Sally having just turned seventeen and Duncan eighteen. "Here, Penny, you may grate the raw potatoes." Penny sat on a stool at the counter and took the grater and three fat yellow potatoes from Sally.

"Ach, well, if the young lady won't pour a sorry soul like myself a cuppa, then I'll do it for her—and one for Miss Sour-Puss as well."

"Sure you will do no such thing. Mrs. Underhill will be waiting on her coffee," said Sally.

Grandma's coffee? Penny thought Grandma would still be asleep at this hour. Yet there, on a tray by the dumb waiter, sat a full coffee service and a croissant. "Is that for Grandma?" Penny's voice was squeaky with surprise.

"It is." Duncan opened the door to the dumb waiter, hoisted the tray onto the shelf inside, and shut the door.

"But it's too early for Grandma to be awake," said Penny. Duncan and Sally both laughed.

"Your grandmother wakes every day at five, lights her own fire, and then goes about her work. I bring her coffee at 5:45 every day, sharp-like," said Duncan.

"What work?" Grandma did a great deal of volunteer work, but she did that during the daytime.

"Your grandmother runs the companies your grandfather built. It's a pity that your grandma wasn't running the war. It would have been over a lot sooner," said Duncan as he peeled off his brown leather kitchen apron and donned his jacket and cuffs.

Grandma was in business! Was Grandma a suffragette? But Grandma did not approve of suffragettes or woman working for money. So if Grandma didn't approve of working, why did she work?

"Back in a jiffy," said Duncan.

"Can I come with you?" Penny jumped off the stool.

"See here, did ya not want to make your father some boxty?" asked Sally.

"I'll be right back. Really I will." Penny shot past Sally and Duncan and raced up the servants' stairs. She heard Duncan bang open the door of the dumb waiter, fiddle with the coffee tray, and then shut the door again. He gave the rope several sharp tugs. Up the coffee service went, between the walls.

Penny reached the little door to the dumb waiter on the second floor, and then stopped.

The coffee service would be far too heavy for her to lift.

Duncan came up behind her. "Right you are, girl, I'll manage this. Just knock on your grandmother's door." Duncan opened the dumb waiter and hoisted the tray up onto his shoulder while Penny gave her grandmother's door three short raps.

"Come in, Duncan," Grandmother called. Penny turned the doorknob. She had only been in Grandma's room once before and she had barely crossed the threshold then.

The room was grand, with a large oriental rug, ornate lamps, plump chairs, a deep soft sofa, and a huge four-poster bed. Grandmother sat at her desk, holding a long, thin silver pen. Her hair, normally wound in a soft bun, was tied back with a black ribbon. It was silver and thick, as thick as Penny's, and cascaded down her back like a stream of sparkling water. She wore a light-blue dressing gown and red Chinese slippers. Surely her grandma was the most elegant grandma in the world!

"Duncan, please look at that fireplace. It has a very poor draw this morning." Grandma spoke without looking up from her papers.

"Good morning, Grandma," Penny said quietly. Startled, her grandma looked to the door.

"Good heavens, Penny, what are you doing up at this hour?"

"I was thinking about Papa coming today, and Maggie and Emily ..." Her words drifted off.

"I see." Grandma looked at Penny thoughtfully, then put down her pen. "Perhaps you could join me for a cup of coffee. Coffee stunts your growth, so we won't make a habit of it. We'll have our coffee in front of the fire, such as it is. Duncan, fetch another cup, if you please."

"I've already taken the liberty, Madam." Sure enough, Penny saw that two cups now sat on the tray, as well as two croissants, a creamer with milk, and a sugar bowl. When had he done that? Duncan placed each cup on its matching saucer and poured the coffee in a steady stream. Penny could see that her cup had more milk than coffee, but it didn't matter a whit. She felt very grown-up.

"You are becoming a more experienced butler every day, Duncan," said Grandmother. Penny darted her eyes to Duncan's face. He grimaced. Grandma had meant it as a compliment, but Duncan didn't take it that way. His plans did not include being *in service* for a lifetime.

"Do sit, Penny. One can't have one's coffee standing up. It's not civilized."

Penny sat down on a chair not far from Grandmother. It was then that she saw it. On the wall, framed in gilded wood, was a portrait of Mama. Penny drew in a sharp breath. Mama would have been about fifteen, maybe sixteen, years old when the picture was painted. She had hair the colour of gold and sparkling blue eyes. Penny could hardly drag her eyes away from the sight of her mother.

"Miss Penny." Duncan handed Penny her cup, along with a napkin, small plate, and croissant.

"Thank you," she mumbled. Duncan gave a slight bow, then left the room.

She must think of something to say—anything would do! "Duncan says that you rise early every day." Penny tried to speak like a lady, but it was a strain to raise her voice above a whisper.

"Your grandfather left us well provided for, but I still have a great deal to do," said Grandma. "I have good managers running the companies, but I like to keep on top of things. And there are the investments and, of course, the regular household accounts for both this house and the house in Halifax. It all takes time."

Companies? Investments? Penny's mouth gaped open. "Grandma, are you a suffragette?" She blurted out the question before she could stop herself.

By the look on Grandma's face, Penny might as well have asked her if she were a circus performer!

"I should say not! Suffragette indeed. We must not forget that a woman's place is in the home, raising a family."

"But why?" Penny didn't know how exactly to ask the questions in her head.

"Why what, my dear?" asked Grandmother as she sipped her coffee.

"Why do you work? Couldn't you, well, sell the companies?" Penny often heard the girls talking at school about their fathers buying and selling companies.

"I have no choice. I simply must keep it all going."

"But why?"

"For you, my dear, and for your sisters. It is your inheritance."

"I don't know how you talked me into this." Grandma, dressed in a mink coat, hat, and long leather gloves, stood in the snow in front of Windsor Station. Penny, wearing a velvet coat with fur trim, and a fur hat, wasn't sure how she had talked Grandmother into letting her meet the trains either. It was, Penny thought, a Christmas miracle.

"Arthur, we shall go directly to the track." Grandmother called out to the aging chauffeur who stood in front of the Cadillac. "Engage one of those public cabs to carry home the luggage

16

and then meet us there." Grandma nodded (it would be rude to point) towards a line of automobiles and two horse-drawn sleighs that were queued up at the corner.

"I was planning to do that, Madam," grumbled Arthur.

"Go along then," said Grandma.

"Yes, ma'am." Arthur rolled his eyes and meandered over to the cab stop. Grandmother mumbled something about packing him off to an old folks' home.

Grandma and Penny went through the great doors of Windsor Station. It was always beautiful, with its glass roof and stone floors. Now it was done up with Christmas decorations, and the red, blue, and white Union Jack hung from every possible post.

"Straighten your hat, Penelope, shoulders back." Penny did as she was told and tried to suppress a giggle. In a few minutes, Papa's train would arrive from Halifax. After that Aunt Colleen, Maggie, and Emily would arrive on a different track from Toronto. Penny could hardly stand it. She tried desperately to stand still.

"You there," Grandmother called to a porter. "Where is the train from Halifax expected to disembark?" The porter pointed to a black iron railing that led to the tracks. Grandmother nodded then turned to Penny. "Remember, deportment is the hallmark of refinement. Private feelings are not meant for public consumption. There is no need to be overly demonstrative. Simply greet your father in a ladylike fashion. From now on, *you* must be your sisters' model of decorum." Grandmother spoke crisply.

"Yes, Grandma," Penny said automatically. She had heard it all before.

The black cone of the train's engine lurched into the station. Penny stood on her tiptoes. Surely Grandmother would not object to tiptoes? *Oh, Papa, hurry.* The train hissed to a stop, the doors banged open, and people flooded out. "Merry Christmas," people called to each other. *"Joyeux Noël."* The English and French languages mixed easily. The crowd began to thin, and Penny wondered if Papa could have slipped by without their seeing him. She stretched her neck to its limit, straining to see. What if Papa had missed the train? The thought made her catch her breath. *Please, please, let him come.* An old lady and boy climbed carefully out of the train, and then there was no one.

Penny looked sideways at Grandma. There was no trace of emotion on Grandmother's face. She stood, as always, regal and tall. A lump formed in Penny's throat. *Don't cry, don't cry.* Penny looked down. What if Aunt Colleen and her sisters didn't arrive either?

It was then, as Penny was looking down at her feet and trying her very best to stifle her tears, that Grandma herself let out a small cry. What was wrong? Penny pivoted on her toes and reached out to her grandmother but—too late. Grandmother lunged forward. Penny looked down the platform and gasped as Grandma called, "Robert!"

Uncle Robert, thin and pale, stood on the platform. A cane propped him up on one side. Beside him stood a man wearing a hat. "Papa!" Penny cried. Grandma and Robert, Penny and Papa stumbled towards each other. Tears gathered in Grandma's eyes. Penny felt herself being lifted high into the air. She squealed with delight.

"Robert! Oh, dear boy, we were so worried. What will Colleen say? Oh, dear boy, are you all right? It's been months. Why didn't you tell us you were coming?" Grandmother was asking all her questions at once.

"I'm fine, Auntie." Uncle Robert gave his auntie a firm hug. The effort seemed to sap his energy. Grandma took out a lace hanky and dabbed her eyes.

"Papa, I thought that you had missed the train." Penny buried her face in the collar of Papa's thick wool coat.

"Sure if I'd missed the train, I'd have run all the way to Montreal." Papa's Irish accent sounded like music to her ears. He set her down and laughed.

Over Papa's shoulder, Penny saw Arthur's mouth gape open. He was staring at the sight of Mrs. Underhill standing in a public place and crying.

"There you all are!" Grandma, Penny, Papa, and Uncle Robert turned and looked into the smiling face of Aunt Colleen. Two-year-old Maggie held one of Aunt Colleen's hands, while six-year-old Emily held the other.

"Maggie! Emily!" Penny cried. Grandma's eyes filled with tears again as she gazed for the first time at her other two granddaughters. In one mighty sweep, Papa hoisted Maggie and Emily up into his arms. As Papa moved, Aunt Colleen caught sight of Robert. She cried out and rushed towards her brother with open arms. Everyone talked and laughed and cried at once, everyone except Maggie, who peered round-eyed at them all. Poor darling baby Maggie. Not a sound had come out of her mouth since the morning of the Halifax explosion. Maggie had simply stopped making noise on December 6, 1917, and here it was December 20, 1918.

"Maggie, Maggie, it's me. It's Penny." Penny gently kissed the two-year-old's cheek before turning to Emily. "Oh, Emily, look how big you are." Papa kept saying, "Ah, my girls, my beautiful wee Irish girls." Uncle Robert, with his arm still around his sister, touched Penny's shoulder. "Uncle Robert," Penny cried. It was her turn to hug her uncle.

"Enough of this. Arthur? Arthur? Where is that man?" Grandma looked about.

"At your service, Madam, as always," he muttered. Grandma jumped.

"Oh, for heaven's sake. I am plagued with servants whose sole intent is to give me a start."

"Yes, Madam."

"Come, let's go home." Like a ship leading the brigade, Grandma marshalled her dignity and marched towards the grand front doors of Windsor Station. The rest followed, arm in arm. Two porters wheeled pushcarts piled high with luggage.

*Everyone talked and laughed
and cried at once.*

A cab was parked behind Grandmother's auto-mobile. Arthur organized the luggage, leaving Grandma to organize the people. "Colleen, Robert, and Mr. Reid, you and the girls will take my car. Penny, you will have to sit up front with Arthur. Mind his driving. He's getting old."

"Thank you, Madam," Arthur added dryly while holding on to the door.

Penny stopped. "But, Grandma, how are you getting home?"

"Do you think me incapable of making my way home in my own city? Good heavens, girl, I am not an antique."

"Of course you are not, Madam," Arthur added. Grandma scowled at him. Colleen and Robert protested. Papa offered to walk or ride in the cab with the luggage.

"Nonsense. Your daughters need you. Colleen, put Maggie on your lap. Penny, don't stand there like a pillar box—in you get. I shall follow behind in the cab. You there, cabbie, open the door." The young cab driver hustled around to the passenger door, opened it, and stood at attention. "I trust your cab is up to snuff."

"No, ma'am. I don't take snuff," said the young cabbie.

"Whatever are you talking about?" Grandma slid into the front seat. "Home, driver."

The cabbie took his seat behind the wheel. "I'm sorry, Madam, I do not know where that is."

"Oh, good heavens," Grandma sighed.

Penny sat beside Arthur in the front while everyone else piled into the backseat, behind the glass that separated the driver from the passengers. Emily leaned forward and whispered to Penny through an opening in the window, "Is Grandma always this scary?"

Penny giggled. "Grandma is the best grandma in the whole world, Emily. The very best. You'll see."

CHAPTER No 3

Cook, Sally, Duncan, and Nancy stood
in the entrance of the great house and peered out
to the drive.

It was Duncan who first glimpsed Grandmother
sitting up front in a cab. "Dear saints in heaven," he
whispered. "Is Mrs. Underhill sitting *on* a suitcase?"

It was all they could do not to cast their eyes
heavenward and say a prayer for sure the world
had turned on its ear.

Arthur stopped behind the cab. Everyone piled
out of the car and into the house, leaving
Duncan and the cabbie to sort out the bags.

Grandmother stood in the entrance, pulled off her gloves, and surveyed her staff. "Good, you are all here. I'm sure you all recognize Captain Robert, and this is Mr. David Reid, Penny's father. These are my grandchildren, Emily and Margaret. And of course we all welcome home Miss Colleen." The staff murmured greetings while Maggie buried her face in the fur collar on Aunt Colleen's coat.

Grandmother introduced each servant by name and then announced that high tea would be served at four o'clock, in the drawing room. Meanwhile, a rest was required. Grandma didn't mention Uncle Robert by name, but clearly it was he who needed to lie down. For the first time, Penny really looked at Uncle Robert. Just a few short months ago, on that dreadful day at Mrs. Meighen's house when she had come down the great staircase with juice spilled down her dress, Robert had been strong enough to swing her up in his arms. Now he seemed delicate and as pale as ice.

Sally was told to make up another bedroom and Duncan was instructed to take Papa and Uncle Robert up to their rooms. Wiry and strong, Duncan picked up the bags and asked the gentlemen to follow him. Penny saw trepidation cross Uncle Robert's face as he gazed up the circular staircase. Aunt Colleen's brow furrowed as she looked first towards her brother and then to Papa. They seemed to exchange thoughts although words were not spoken.

"Penny, take care of your sisters while I help Robert to his room," Papa said quietly and kindly. Penny extended her hand towards her six-year-old sister. "Come on, Emily, I'll show you to your room."

"Oh, one moment, Mr. Reid," Grandmother called after Penny's father. "Would you mind coming down fifteen minutes early? I have something to discuss with you."

Penny spun around. Grandma wanted to talk to Papa *in secret*? Whatever for? It had to be about her.

Papa nodded and then added, "I'd be pleased if you called me David."

"Very well," said Grandma rather stiffly. "I'll see you promptly at 3:45—David." Papa and Uncle Robert lumbered up the stairs after Duncan.

"Colleen, spare me a moment," said Grandmother as she walked into the drawing room. Maggie immediately clung harder to Aunt Colleen. She was as wide-eyed and frightened as a baby rabbit.

"Maggie, darling, take Penny's hand. I will just have a word with your grandma and then I will come up to your room." Aunt Colleen set Maggie down and whispered into the two-year-old's ear.

"It's okay, Maggie, come with Emily and me," said Penny. "I'll show you your room. There are lots of toys waiting for you." Maggie's lower lip quivered as she reached for Emily's hand. "She doesn't remember me," said Penny softly.

"Yes she does. Everything is coming at her too fast, that's all." Aunt Colleen gave Maggie a big hug and said, "Penny has missed you so much. She will take you upstairs. Up you go. I'll be along soon." Reluctantly and with tears in her eyes, Maggie trudged up the stairs with Emily and Penny.

They reached the first floor, walked down the hall, and opened the door to the biggest guest room in the house. They stopped just inside, and Emily sucked in her breath. Maggie's blue eyes grew round as berries. Neither moved. "Come on." Penny urged. The girls would not budge.

"What's that?" Emily pointed to Mama's old dollhouse.

"It's yours. And look, Maggie, here's Mama's rocking horse." Penny ran her hand over its golden mane. "Nice horsey. Come pat it. See the teddy bears and the toys in the toy box?" Maggie stood behind Emily, shut her eyes, and covered her ears. "What's wrong?" Penny's own eyes were wide with alarm. She thought that her sisters would howl with delight. They hadn't even noticed the games, blocks, and books.

"Maggie, don't be scared." Emily hugged her sister while Penny just stood and watched. Why was Maggie scared? And why did Maggie rush to Emily and not her? But Penny knew why: Emily was the big sister now, not her.

"What's all this then?" Sally stood in the doorway holding a tray with two mugs of warm milk and a plate of cookies. "Oh, I see. It's a bit much after such a journey. Let's get you unpacked and out of those clothes. I imagine a cup of hot milk and a nap will fix things up." Penny edged outside the room and watched as Sally took charge.

Penny walked down the hall towards her own room, biting her lip. Naps—she should have thought of that. Maybe it was possible to forget how to be a big sister. She stopped in front of Papa's room, listening, and opened the door a crack. "Papa, are you sleeping?" she whispered.

"Penny." Papa swung open the door and smiled.

Penny flung her arms around her father. "Oh, Papa, I am so happy to see you. I prayed and prayed that you would come for Christmas. It worked!"

"Now, darlin', let me look at yea. You're a picture. What do they feed you in this province? You're taller by half!" There was nothing to cry about, but tears rolled down Penny's face anyway.

"What's this? Come sit down." Papa pulled up two chairs, then took Penny's hands in his and looked into her eyes. "Now tell me, what are the tears about?"

Penny rubbed her eyes with her fists. "Nothing. It's just … Emily is so big and Maggie …"

"I know. They are growing up without you. Is that it?"

"How did you know?"

"Because I feel the same way. Look at you— you are a young lady. Another six months and I wouldn't know you. Are you happy here, darlin'? Sure it's a grand house."

Happy? Penny sniffed and swallowed a hiccup. How should she answer that? She really liked her school, and she did love Grandma and

Aunt Colleen, and she had lots of friends now. She was happy, but if she said that to Papa, would he think that she didn't love him any more? If she told him that she was unhappy, might he say something that would hurt Grandma's feelings?

She shrugged. Papa grew thoughtful for a moment and then asked her about her friends. It was easy to tell him about Gwen.

"Excuse me, sir." Duncan stood at the door. "Miss Colleen would like a word with you in the upstairs sitting room when you have a moment."

"Thank you, Duncan," Papa said politely. "My daughter can show me the way." Duncan gave a slight nod of his head and left.

"It's just down the hall." Penny jumped up. She was relieved, although it was hard to explain why. She led Papa down the long hall to the upstairs sitting room. Aunt Colleen would never have thought of coming to Papa's room. A lady never, ever sat with a man in his bedroom even if the door was left wide open!

The upstairs sitting room was filled with lush plants, big stuffed chairs, and books. A bright fire burned in the grate.

"There you are, David," Aunt Colleen turned from the fire. Her face was flushed from its heat. She looked extra pretty.

"My guide led the way," said Papa.

Aunt Colleen smiled at Penny. "Come in, both of you."

Penny shook her head and politely excused herself. It was funny, but she wanted to be alone. And she couldn't explain that either!

The clock chimed the quarter hour. Penny checked on Emily and Maggie but ducked out before they could see her. Sally was getting the girls up from their naps. Uncle Robert's door was ajar. He was lying on his bed with a rug over his legs. Aunt Colleen was sitting by his bed. The two were talking quietly. Duncan was likely in the kitchen helping Cook and Nancy with the tea.

Penny quietly opened the door to the servants' stairs. She darted inside, removed her shoes, and placed them side by side on the second step. There was no telling the trouble she'd get into if she were caught eavesdropping, but she *had* to know why Grandma wanted to talk to Papa privately. It must be about her, it just *had* to be.

She didn't dare turn on the stairwell lights. Instead, she held tightly to the banister and felt her way down the dark steps. A thin sliver of light shone from under the door—the secret door to the drawing room. It wasn't really a secret—everyone who lived and worked in the house knew it was there. In the old days, servants used the back stairs to carry coal and wood, buckets of soapy water, and rug sweepers, and to deliver meals too. It was as if another world lived behind the walls.

Penny eased open the door just a crack. She had a good view of Grandma at her desk. The main door to the drawing room opened.

"Please come in and close the door, David. And do help yourself to a glass of sherry," said Grandma. Papa politely refused. "I trust you know about this?"

Grandma held up a piece of paper. Could that paper be her marks from the Christmas exams?

Papa's arm came into view. He reached over and took the paper from Grandma.

"I am grateful that you arranged the test," said Papa absently as he read the letter in his hand. Which test? There had been many—mathematics, geography, algebra, grammar, English literature, French, Greek, Latin. Latin was a hateful subject.

"There is nothing wrong with her physically. Stability is what the child requires," said Grandma.

What did they mean? She was stable. What more stability could anyone offer?

"I understand," replied Papa as he handed Grandma back the letter.

What did Papa understand? Oh, this was agony.

"The child needs permanence. I'm sure your sister is doing her very best, but she has children of her own. Colleen mentioned that there is another baby on the way."

Another baby? Of course! Grandma and Papa weren't talking about her. They were talking about Maggie. Grandma had asked Aunt Colleen to find a doctor in Toronto who would examine Maggie to find out why she wouldn't, or couldn't, talk. But what did this have to do with *permanence?* Maybe the doctor had said that Maggie wouldn't start talking until she had a *permanent* home!

"Yes, I have been giving the matter some thought," said Papa.

"So have I," interjected Grandma. "Forgive me, but they are my grandchildren and naturally I want what's best for them. You can see how Penny has flourished here. She doesn't know it yet, but Miss Potter tells me that Penny has achieved three *firsts* this semester. Remarkable when you consider how academically behind she was when she arrived. I have also inquired about space for Emily at the school. She could begin after Christmas. As for Maggie, you can be assured that she will get the best medical help."

What was happening? Was Grandma saying that all three of them would live in Montreal *forever?* What about Papa?

"You must see that this is a sensible suggestion, David. You are a young man with a future ahead of you. I have heard from a variety of sources that your company is flourishing. You are well on your way to becoming very successful. No man of your age wants to be encumbered by three small girls."

Encumbered? Was she a burden to her father? If only she could see his face.

"My future includes my children."

"That is to your credit, David, but I simply ask that you consider what's best for them. Penny misses her sisters and I assume they miss her. They would be together again in a good home. They would have social standing. Young ladies need a woman's influence. Think of their manners! Then there is the matter of their education. Miss Potter's School for Girls offers the finest education in the country. There's no telling where they could go after that—McGill perhaps, or Cambridge or Oxford. Elizabeth was very keen on education."

The mention of Mama's name seemed to take the wind out of Papa's sails. It was true that Mama had always hoped that her girls would go as far in school as they wanted. "And Emily and Maggie have certainly taken to Colleen. She is more than an aunt to Penny, she's more like a ..." Grandma's voice faded.

"She's more like a mother," Papa finished Grandma's sentence. He paused and then took a deep breath. "There is nothing you have said that I have not considered. I am grateful for all your help. I don't have to tell you that the threat of contagious diseases after the explosion was very real. I am forever in your debt for taking in Penny. And my company is, as you say, flourishing. I plan to start building the new house in the spring. It will be ready in time for the new school year."

Penny held her breath. Grandmother wasn't used to people saying no to her. "Might I suggest that we leave it for now? We have the holidays to look forward to. We could discuss it after

Christmas," said Grandma in a voice that sounded distant and cool.

"With all due respect, the matter is closed. I want my family back."

There was silence for what felt like a very long time. "I see. Would you allow me some time to myself before the family comes down?"

"Yes, of course." Papa moved away and now Penny could see Grandma clearly. Her jaw was set, her shoulders square, her head high.

"Mrs. Underhill, I really am most grateful." Papa, like a true gentleman, bowed his head with respect. In regal fashion, Grandma returned the nod.

Alone now, Grandma went to the window and looked out at the falling snow. Penny watched as her grandmother's shoulders sagged and her head drooped. In an instant, Grandma had shrunk into an old woman. Penny leaned her head against the doorjamb and tried not to cry.

As the door opened again, Grandma straightened and turned. "Robert, there you are. Do help yourself to some sherry. I believe Duncan also put out something stronger. Where is your sister?"

"She's with the girls. I believe that there's a mad hunt on for Penny," said Robert.

Penny backed away from the door, turned, then ran up the stairs. She had had the good sense to put on her best dress before coming down, but she'd have some explaining to do if Sally got hold of her now. It was just as well that Penny was in a panic. She didn't want to think about the conversation she had overheard. After all, it was good news. Papa was making plans for them all to be together again. It was exactly what she had wished for. But if it was good news, why did she feel so awful?

CHAPTER N.º 5

Penny took the back stairs two by two. It didn't matter that it was dark or that she could have easily stumbled. What mattered was not getting caught eavesdropping on Grandma and Papa's conversation.

She slipped on her shoes and popped out of the upstairs servants' door just before Aunt Colleen came out of the girls' bedroom. "Penny, we've been looking for you."

Emily, all smiles and bobbing curls, ran up to Penny. Martha, Mama's doll, was in her arms. "Where did you get that?" Penny demanded.

She hadn't meant to snap.

"That's my fault, Penny. I sent Emily into your room to look for you, and she spotted Martha on your bed. I hope you don't mind," said Aunt Colleen as she straightened the bow in Maggie's thick blond hair. Strangely enough, Penny did mind. There was a roomful of toys and dolls and stuffed teddy bears for Emily to pick from. Why did she want Martha? "Come along, girls, everyone will be waiting." Aunt Colleen took Maggie's hand and the two slowly walked ahead of Emily and Penny.

Penny waited until Aunt Colleen and Maggie were halfway down the stairs before gently reaching for Martha. "Why don't we go back to your room and get a different doll, Emily?"

Emily tightened her hold on the doll. "No!" The small smile faded and in its place was a fierce look, complete with pursed lips.

"But there are lots of nice toys to choose from. Let's go look at the jack-in-the-box. There's a spinner, too."

"No!" This time Emily put Martha behind her back.

"Penny, Emily, where did you get to? Downstairs, the pair of you. Duncan will be bringing in the tea in a minute," said Sally as she barged down the hall. She might have stopped to quiz Penny further about her whereabouts had she not had to get down to the kitchen.

"You can keep Martha but just for *now*. Promise that you'll give her back?" whispered Penny into Emily's ear. Emily bobbed her head. "Come on then," said Penny.

"There you two are," said Grandma as Penny and Emily entered the drawing room. She was sitting in one of the large Queen Anne chairs by the fire.

Papa and Aunt Colleen sat on the settee with Maggie between them. Emily plunked herself down on the floor, crossed her legs, and played with Martha while Uncle Robert poured something gold into a crystal tumbler—whiskey perhaps. Grandma hardly ever served alcohol, and never with children present, but maybe she was making an exception because of Uncle Robert and Papa.

"I thought the girls would like to go up to Beaver Lake on the mountain tomorrow and skate. It's quite safe now that the lake is frozen. You could take a horse-drawn sleigh around Mount Royal too. What do you say, Emily?" Grandma spoke kindly to her second granddaughter. Penny knew that Emily hadn't the faintest idea what Grandma was talking about, but all the adults seemed to think it was a good idea, and so Emily nodded. "Good. I'll call Maitlands and have skates delivered in the morning. Colleen, do ask Sally to measure the girls' feet."

With glass in hand, Robert eased himself into a chair across from Grandma just as Duncan rolled in the tea wagon. Sally followed, carrying a three-tiered cake-and-sandwich stand, then scooted about, setting up little tea tables. A lace doily went on each table, followed by a small plate and napkin.

"I'll pour if you like, Aunt Penelope," suggested Aunt Colleen. Grandma gave her a nod. Duncan rolled the tea wagon in front of Aunt Colleen. She picked up a delicate teacup and saucer in one hand and lifted the heavy teapot in the other. Not a bit of strain showed on her face. One thing was certain: Penny would never be as elegant as Aunt Colleen.

"Beg your pardon, sir, but these were made especially for you by Miss Penny." Sally stood in front of Papa holding out a plate of sliced, hot boxty bread. Papa's eyebrows shot up in surprise. He reached for a piece, added butter, and took a bite.

"And a better piece of boxty can't be had no matter what side of the great pond I may be on." He looked over at his daughter with pride. Penny blushed. Truly, it was Sally who had made the potato bread. Everyone tried a piece, even Grandma.

"David and I checked on your house in Halifax, Aunt Penelope," said Robert. "The windows that were repaired last winter are all fine, no leaks or drafts. The damage done to the west side of Halifax during the explosion was minimal. Nevertheless, David checked out the foundation and structure."

"I would value your professional opinion, David," said Grandma to Papa.

"As I said to Colleen on her last visit to Halifax, a house is a living thing," said Papa. "It requires constant attention. The basic structure is solid but there are things to be attended to before real problems set in, the roof for example."

"Would you make me up a list?"

"I'd be pleased to, but have no fear, the house itself will stand for a hundred years. It's a fine piece of work."

"Papa, you should see Mrs. Meighen's house. It's down on Drummond Street. Oh, Papa, you would love it," Penny gushed.

"Ah, that reminds me. Robert, Mrs. Meighen rang up while you were resting. She is delighted to hear that you are back. I invited her over for tea tomorrow afternoon, perhaps after skating."

Robert nodded. "Thank you, Aunt Penelope, but I'm not up to ice skating just yet. I would, however, be delighted to see Mrs. Meighen," he said as he set down his glass. Mrs. Elsie Meighen and Grandmother were not only the oldest of friends but also the two most power-ful women in Montreal. Exhaustion seemed to envelop Robert and he turned quite pale. Grandma looked at him with concern. "Perhaps we should ask Dr. Sanders to pay us a call," suggested Grandma. Uncle Robert shook his head vehemently. No doctor. He was on the mend, he said.

It didn't seem fair that Uncle Robert was so ill. A shell had taken off half his foot, which was why he walked with a cane. He could have left the army after his injury but instead he had become an *aide-de-camp*. That meant he assisted another officer but did not see battle. "Did you know that if it were not for this man, I'd not be sitting with you now?" Uncle Robert nodded in Papa's direction.

"You exaggerate," said Papa quietly.

"Do I?" Uncle Robert laughed. "Hours after peace was declared on November 11, I was given orders to demobilize and report to Ottawa as soon as possible. I left France, took an ambulance ship across the channel to England, and boarded the first ship home to Halifax. The influenza struck the second day out to sea. Half the men on the ship came down with it. Once we docked, those who could still walk were put on trains. I shudder to think of the spread of this disease." Aunt Colleen let out a soft moan. This was exactly how the flu was spreading—soldiers boarding trains with this deadly influenza were fanning out across Canada.

"The hospital in Halifax was already filled to capacity. It was David who took me in. Many are turning their backs on the soldiers sick with influenza. They're afraid of catching it themselves. I don't recall your father ever being afraid." Robert looked to Penny then to Papa. His eyes were filled with admiration.

"David, thank you." Aunt Colleen reached across Maggie and laid her hand over Papa's. Penny thought that she might burst with pride.

"Well, David, it seems that this family is in your debt," said Grandma.

"There is no debt," Papa said firmly. Maggie climbed up onto his lap and laid her head on his shoulder. *I wish that were me,* thought Penny. *I wish I was little again so that I could sit on Papa's lap and fall asleep on his shoulder too.*

"I have numb-bum," announced Emily.

"I beg your pardon!" Grandma's eyebrows shot up.

"I can't feel my bum. It's numb. Numb-bum."

Uncle Robert looked as if he was about to pop his buttons with laughter. Aunt Colleen covered her mouth and tried (with limited success) to muffle her giggles. Papa looked confused, and Grandma was simply horrified!

"Emily, come with me." Penny grabbed hold of the six-year-old's hand and pulled. The two stopped outside the drawing room. Penny shut the door behind them and looked down at her sister.

"Who taught that word to you?"

"Shamus."

"Who is Shamus?"

"He's our cousin. He's nine. He knows lots of things."

Just like Billy Hanson, thought Penny. "Has he taught you any other words?"

"No, but he says that we are orphans. Are we orphans?"

"No, we are not. Is Shamus mean to you?" Oh, Penny could cheerfully give this cousin of hers a piece of her mind!

"No. He just wants his bed back. There's no room in Aunt Tilly's house, so Shamus has to sleep in the hall."

Penny's anger melted away. There are two sides to everything. "Emily, you must listen to me carefully. You must never say that word again. Promise?"

"What word?"

"The *bum* word." Penny lowered her voice.

"You said it. You said it! Penny said the b-word. Penny said the b-word." Emily danced as she sang.

"EMILY!" Penny had forgotten just how exasperating six-year-olds were.

CHAPTER N.º 6

December 22

Lots of people were skating on Beaver Lake on this winter day, and even more people were standing on the snowbanks and watching, or sitting on spindly chairs and drinking cocoa. Christmas was only three days away, and everyone was in a festive mood.

Despite Aunt Colleen's protests, Uncle Robert had come with them, although he wasn't actually skating. He was wrapped in a fur blanket and sitting in the back of a horse-drawn sleigh beside the lake. Once in a while he'd smile and wave, but most of the time he seemed to be staring into the distance.

Gwen had also joined the skating party. Ducking and weaving past slower skaters, Penny caught up to her. "Here, take my hand." Gwen grabbed hold of Penny's hand and the two went gliding across the ice. They both howled with laughter then screamed, "Look out!" Thunk. Both girls landed in a snowbank and laughed even harder. Gwen rolled over on her back and dusted off the snow but made no attempt to get up.

"He's handsome." Gwen gazed over at Papa. Penny looked too. Papa and Aunt Colleen were both wearing skates. Maggie, who was between them, had cheese-cutters strapped to her boots.

Aunt Colleen, wearing a dark red velvet coat and a black fur hat, looked dramatic and elegant against the white ice and snow. She held Papa's arm tightly since he was not a strong skater.

"Your aunt is sweet on your father. He likes her too. I have a nickel. Do you want a hot

Gwen grabbed hold of Penny's hand and the two went gliding across the ice.

chocolate?" Gwen spoke absent-mindedly as she sat up and brushed the rest of the snow off her coat.

Penny lay as she had landed, her back against the snowbank, her skates still on the ice. "What did you just say?"

"Here I come!" Emily came flying across the ice and landed between the two girls. Gwen moaned. Emily had accidentally whacked her under the chin. "I'm sorry, Ben," mumbled Emily, who lay face down in the snow.

"It's Gwen and that's okay." Even though Emily was only six and Gwen almost thirteen, the two got on well. Gwen kept telling Penny how lucky she was to have sisters. Being an only child was awful.

"I said, what did you say?" Penny repeated herself.

"I have a nickel—"

"No, about my aunt Colleen and my father."

"I said that your aunt and your father like each other," said Gwen.

"Of course they like each other. They have known each other for years and years." Penny was annoyed.

"I don't mean *like* as in *like,* I mean like as in *more* than like." Gwen seemed pleased with her observation. Emily flipped over on her back and the three girls stared at the couple skating on the bumpy, cracked ice. Aunt Colleen's cheeks were red with the cold and her eyes, normally so gentle and mild, now sparkled with excitement. And Papa didn't look the least bit tired any more.

Could it be true? Penny's heart raced. Papa and Aunt Colleen had left the house early this morning to do some Christmas shopping. No children allowed, they had said, then off they went. At lunch the two had returned home laden with boxes and bags. Penny hadn't been the least bit suspicious at the time, but thinking back, they did look happy together.

Penny scrambled up onto her skates and pushed off. At first she skated slowly then gradually picked up the pace. Without thinking, Penny was skating as fast as she possibly could. Faster, faster until everyone became a blur as she passed. Arms extended, she crossed one skate over the other as she took the curves. Small children scattered and older ones applauded. As she sped across the ice, thoughts raced around in her brain. Aunt Colleen and Papa were always writing to each other and Aunt Colleen had even gone to Halifax to check on Grandma's house. She had met Papa when she was there. Papa said so himself just yesterday. Could they have fallen in love?

"Look out!" The warning came too late. Penny screamed, put her hands out in front of her, and then crashed into a wooden board that had been placed in front of a small statue in the middle of the ice.

Sally opened the door. "Dear heaven, what's happened?" She stood on tiptoes and looked at Penny as she lay wrapped in a blanket in Papa's arms.

"What's this?" Grandma flung open the drawing room door and came running, actually running, across the hall.

"Penny fell down," announced Emily. Everyone, Aunt Colleen, Uncle Robert, Maggie, Emily, even Gwen, piled into the front entrance behind Papa and Penny. Skates clattered on the stone floor and snow from boots made instant puddles.

"Bring her in. Never mind your boots." Grandma led them all into the drawing room. At that moment Penny and Grandma were exactly the same colour, both as grey as cement. "Sally, send for the doctor," Grandma shouted, actually shouted!

"Really, Grandma, I'm fine," mumbled Penny. And she was fine although suffering from acute embarrassment. Everyone was making such a fuss.

Papa lay Penny down on a sofa and touched her head. "How is your eyesight?" he asked gently.

"Fine, Papa, really. I'm fine."

Papa smiled. "I think you'll have a couple of bruises," he said.

"Are you sure, are you absolutely sure she's fine?" Grandma's hands were clutched together and her brow was furrowed into ridges. Papa nodded again. "What happened?"

"It was my fault, Grandma. I was skating too fast and wasn't watching where I was going."

"Careless, just careless. You could have been seriously hurt." Grandma was quite distraught.

"She's as strong as you are, Penelope. It will take more than a spill to hurt your granddaughter." Mrs. Meighen, standing by the window, had watched the entire scene with interest.

"Maybe so, but a bad break can cause lifelong problems. Sally? Oh, where is that girl?" Grandmother went off in search of Sally, and for a brief moment, everyone was occupied. There were skates and coats to be dealt with. Emily and Maggie still had their boots on. Gwen couldn't find her glove. Papa had returned to the hall to remove his own galoshes and Robert along with him. Duncan came in and created more confusion by piling the coats, scarves, hats, and gloves into a jumble.

Mrs. Meighen looked around, took in the friendly chaos, then turned and smiled down at the girl on the sofa. "My dear, I must say that you have brought a great deal of cheer to this house. I haven't seen my old friend as happy as this since ..." Mrs. Meighen stopped talking and patted Penny's hand. "It is lovely that you are in all our lives, but especially in your grandmother's."

Penny's eyes widened. Happy? Grandma didn't seem the least bit happy. Upset, anxious, worried— but not happy! And what did she mean—*since when*? But Penny knew what Mrs. Meighen was thinking. Mrs. Meighen was going to say that she hadn't seen Grandma this happy since Mama was alive.

"Robert." Mrs. Meighen greeted him as he entered the drawing room again. Aunt Colleen,

Papa, and Grandma followed. Then came the introductions. Duncan had poured sherry for the ladies and whiskey for the gentlemen. It took a few minutes before everyone settled down.

"Why on earth were you skating so fast?" asked Grandma. Penny twisted the corner of the blanket. She didn't dare look in Gwen's direction.

"Gwen said that Papa and Aunt Colleen were sweet on each other." Emily said it just like that, as bold as you please.

Not a word was spoken or a breath taken, although had anyone noticed they would have seen a small smile on Uncle Robert's face.

It was Gwen who broke the silence. "I'm sorry. I didn't actually say that. I mean I shouldn't have … I am sorry." Gwen's face glowed. She fumbled about, mumbled something about being expected home, and then bolted for the door.

Penny looked across the room. Papa and Aunt Colleen were staring at each other. There it was again. It was as if they were talking to each other without saying any words.

Mrs. Meighen, who seemed to take everything in graciously, took her leave. "Do come by and see me, Robert. I would like the pleasure of your company before you resume your duties in Ottawa." And to Papa she said, "Your daughters are charming, and I would indeed like to better know the man who raised them." Papa stood and shook Mrs. Meighen's hand.

"Allow me to walk you to the door," said Grandma, who rose from her chair slowly. She looked tired.

Aunt Colleen, who looked a little bewildered, suggested that they all retire to their rooms to get dressed for dinner. Sally took that moment to pop out of the wall, startling everyone but Aunt Colleen and Penny. Even Papa jumped! Papa looked at the secret door with great interest.

"Hot chocolate, how thoughtful," said Aunt Colleen to Sally. "I think it best if you take it up to the girls' room. Perhaps they can have a nursery dinner there tonight as well."

With the tray balanced perfectly in her hands, Sally led the girls from the room. Uncle Robert and Aunt Colleen followed, and Penny trailed behind. She wanted to get away and think.

"Penny, I'd like to talk to you," Papa said.

The door closed behind Aunt Colleen. They were alone. Penny walked to the window and there she stood, glum and sullen.

It was getting dark early now. She could see Papa's reflection in the window. "No! Don't, Papa!" she cried. Penny whirled and dove past him. "Martha! You were about to sit on Martha." Penny picked up the doll and buried her face in the doll's hair. All her dreams of the best Christmas ever were gone. For a minute neither spoke, and then Penny asked in a small, thin voice, "Do you love Aunt Colleen?" She asked the question bravely, but before it was entirely said, she felt herself grow hot with embarrassment.

"Yes, I do."

She didn't have to ask if Aunt Colleen loved him back. "Will you marry her?" Penny set

Martha on the sofa and arranged the doll's dress so that it fanned out prettily.

Papa sat back down on the sofa and ran his hands through his hair. "Darlin', I could not ask her even though I want to. Sure, I haven't a proper home to offer any of yeas at the minute. But there is something I want you to know. I am not trying to replace your mother. I loved your mother more than my life. Do you remember what we talked about that morning before the explosion?"

Penny did, almost every word. But she shook her head and thought, *Tell me again, Papa. Tell me about my mother because she is slipping away.*

When Papa spoke, his voice was low and soft. "My own parents in Ireland died one after the other, leaving six of us wee ones. My sister, your aunt Tilly in Toronto, and I were the oldest, and so we were put on a ship and sent to Canada to work. The others, three boys and a girl, were scattered about the family. When my sister and I arrived in this country, we were two terrified orphans. Many children in our position were beaten and thought of as free labour, but our foster parents were good people. We worked hard and we studied hard. Your aunt met a good man and moved to Toronto. And I met your mother. She was more beautiful than I could ever describe in words and the beauty was both inside and out. And when I held my baby daughters in my arms, I knew that I had found heaven on earth. I knew how to work and I knew how to study, but it was your dear mother who taught me how to live. Would ya have me turn my back on all that she gave me?"

"Oh, Papa. You don't understand. It's not that, it's ..." Penny looked up. Grandma was standing in the doorway. How long had she been there? Papa stood and turned too. Grandma's and Papa's eyes were locked.

"Penny, I'd like to talk to your father," said Grandma. Her voice was not so much hard as it was stern and maybe a bit weary as well. Penny dashed past Papa and Grandma and ran out of the room and up the stairs. She came to a sudden stop on the upstairs landing. Martha—she had forgotten Martha in the drawing room. More than anything, she wanted to hold Mama's doll. Penny leaned over the banister. Grandma had closed the doors to the drawing room. It was too late to retrieve the doll.

CHAPTER № 7

December 23

A whole day had passed since Penny's accident. Maggie and Emily were playing in their room and since there was little else to do, at least nothing she wanted to do, Penny had come to her special place in the attic with the intention of reading a story from *Girl's Own*. She read one story, then two, and then daydreamed for a bit. She wasn't hiding. She just wanted to be alone with her thoughts. Penny sighed as she finally left the attic. Sally would come looking for her if she didn't get back soon.

The upstairs of the house was strangely silent. Penny peeked into the bedrooms, checked the upstairs sitting room. Maggie and Emily were nowhere to be seen. She hopped down the stairs and landed on two feet, at the bottom.

"Penny, is that you?" Grandma called out from the drawing room. Penny wheeled around and crossed the entrance hall to stand in the doorway of the drawing room. Maggie, Emily, Aunt Colleen, Robert, even Mrs. Meighen, stared back at her intently.

"Penny, your father is looking for you," said Grandma.

"Why?" Penny was astonished. Everyone, except Emily and Maggie, looked uncomfortable.

"There have been a few changes in our Christmas plans," Grandma continued. Penny looked from face to face. Changes? What kind of changes? Christmas was Christmas. How could anyone change Christmas?

"I'll go and find David. He should be the one to tell her," said Aunt Colleen. She had a strained, worried look on her face.

"No, tell her now, tell her now!" Emily jumped up and clapped her hands. "We're going home," squealed Emily. "All of us, right after New Year's. We're going home to Halifax and we're going to live in a big house and we're all going to be together forever and ever."

"What are you talking about?" Penny sputtered.

It was Grandma who spoke first. "Well, the cat's out of the bag," sighed Grandma. "Penny, I have given my house in Halifax to your father and Colleen as a wedding gift." Grandmother's words seemed suspended in midair. House? Grandma gave away her *house*? WEDDING?

"It's a big house!" Emily cried.

"Emily, that's enough, sweetheart." Papa stood in the doorway. Penny looked from Papa to Aunt Colleen to Grandma.

"But what has this to do with Christmas?" Penny whispered with a sense of foreboding.

"It's about school, dear," said Aunt Colleen. School?

"Penny, Colleen and I are to be married here, in this house, tomorrow night. We will all be back in Halifax in time for you to start the new year at your old school."

Aunt Colleen and Papa were to be married tomorrow night? But that was Christmas Eve! Surely no one could put together a wedding in a day and a half. Penny looked at Grandma. If anyone could do it, Grandma could.

Penny would have a new mother in two days. She would not return to Miss Potter's School for Girls. She would not learn Latin, or Greek, or the classics. It was happening again. Decisions about her life were being made without anyone asking how she felt. What could she do? She could scream and yell and kick something. She could run up the stairs and throw herself on the bed. She could get angry. She could cry, "It's not fair!"

"I think it's wonderful," whispered Penny.

She felt as if she had been punched in the stomach.

"A wedding! When?" Sally's mouth gaped open.

"Tomorrow night," said Penny. She hadn't exactly sneaked out of the drawing room but she hadn't asked to be excused either.

"Christmas Eve!" Sally looked as if she were about to faint. She sat heavily on the bench beside the kitchen table and pressed her palms against her forehead. "Sure I dinna' want to be the one to tell Cook." Just the thought of Cook's reaction made Sally peer over her shoulder and gaze at Cook's closed bedroom door.

As Penny nodded, a new thought popped into her head. After tomorrow night, her *aunt* would become her *mother.* Was she supposed to call Aunt Colleen Mother?

"Where be they now?" asked Sally.

"Pardon?" Penny was deep in thought.

"The family? Sure, how can we run a house if we don't know what's expected of us?" Sally seemed miffed.

"Papa and Uncle Robert have gone to see about their suits. Aunt Colleen put Maggie and Emily down for their naps. I think she went to Holt's to see about a dress."

"Where is Cook?" Duncan barged into the kitchen.

"Having a nap," replied Sally.

"Rouse her. We're all to go up to the drawing room. Nancy is to come too. Come on, the lot of ya." Duncan was the footman but he was acting like a bossy butler again.

"Right then," said Sally. "I expect this is about the wedding."

"What's that then?" Duncan turned around sharp-like.

"You'll find out soon enough," said Sally as she winked at Penny. "I'll just knock on Cook's door."

Cook was none too happy about being stirred from her nap. She charged up the steps, pausing half way up to catch her breath. "All I ask is peace and quiet twice a day. Is that asking too much?" Sally, Nancy, and Penny, all of whom were trailing Cook, muttered something that sounded like agreement.

Duncan, who had bolted ahead, stood in the hall at the drawing room door. Only when Arthur had arrived did Duncan swing open the door. Grandma, sitting at her desk, motioned for them to enter. "Come, come," she said. Penny trooped along and, not knowing what else to do, darted over to the window seat.

"Penny, there's no need for you to be here but stay if you wish. Gather around. I am pleased to announce the engagement of my niece, Miss Colleen, to Mr. David Reid." Grandma paused as heads bobbed although none knew if this was good or bad news.

"Congratulations, ma'am," said Duncan on behalf of them all.

"Thank you, Duncan. The nuptials and small family reception will take place here, tomorrow

night, which, as you are all aware, is Christmas
Eve. We can expect between sixteen and twenty
guests." Grandma did not pause or acknowledge
the stunned looks. "The ceremony will take place
at six o'clock, officiated by Reverend Munsen.
A light dinner will follow. Cook, if you would,
please prepare a menu for my approval within the
hour. Duncan, we will talk about the wine after
the menu is set, but see that the champagne is put
on ice. The family will have Christmas breakfast
together and open the gifts before Miss Colleen
and Mr. Reid leave on Christmas Day for a brief
stay in New York. They will be returning on
December 31 to pick up the girls and leave for
Halifax on January 2. Miss Penny and Miss Emily
must be in school in Halifax by January 6. Does
anyone have any questions so far?" Grandma
looked from one glum face to the next.

Only when Grandma said that everyone would
receive a bonus for the extra effort did the mood
in the room change. There was talk of the
wedding cake, flowers, pianist, and harpist. On

and on went the list. So there it was. Penny stared out the window. Snowflakes smacked against the glass. Her life was all mapped out and no one had said a word to her.

"I have contacted the agency for more household help. Meanwhile, Duncan, I'd like you to formally take over the butler's duties. Naturally, I will help you with the budgeting and wine cellar, but this too you will eventually take over."

The staff, lead by Sally, all murmured congratulations. Cook, for one, looked plainly shocked. She had said before that Duncan was far too young to be a butler in a large house. It was scandalous. Penny turned and looked intently at Duncan. If he was pleased, he did not show it. In fact, he looked rather sad.

"Arthur? Where is Arthur?" asked Grandma.

Arthur was too old to be standing about and had seated himself in the wing chair by the fire. "There you are," Grandma ignored his lack of propriety. "Tomorrow evening you and Duncan will leave for Verdun at 4:00 sharp." Both Arthur and Duncan were taken aback. Why on earth would they be going to Verdun?

"I neglected to tell you, Duncan, that your mother is an invited guest to the wedding. Given her disability, your attendance is also requested. I have ordered you a new suit and asked the agency to send a butler to stand in for you."

Duncan looked as if his head were swimming. "My—my m-mother, ma'am?" He couldn't stop himself from stammering.

"I will send an invitation to your mother by messenger. It seems that my granddaughter is very fond of your mother, is that not true, Penny?" Penny nodded dumbly. "Your aunt Colleen has specifically asked that your friends attend. I have telephoned Gwendolyn Parker-Jones. She will be accompanied by her mother. Now, there was someone else that Colleen suggested, a professor, what was his name?"

"Dr. Finn helped me with my essay on

Ireland, remember? I was hoping that he might meet Mrs. O'Malley one day ..." Penny's voice faded.

"If you wish he shall be invited to the wedding. No doubt the invitation will come as somewhat of a surprise, but no matter."

Penny nodded. "Grandma, may I invite someone else?"

"I don't see why not. Another friend from school, perhaps?"

"She's here, Grandma. I'd like Sally to come."

The room fell silent, except for Cook's sharp intake of breath.

"Oh, no, ma'am. I dinna think ..." Sally turned pink.

Penny had never seen Sally so vexed. Whatever was wrong? Penny looked to Grandma for help. Grandma sighed and turned to face Sally squarely.

"Sally, we request your attendance at the wedding of Miss Colleen to Mr. David Reid," said Grandma formally.

Sally twisted like a sapling in a storm. It was one thing to serve the upper class but something else entirely to socialize with them!

"Sally, we are waiting." Grandma spoke with uncharacteristic patience.

"The little ones, Miss Maggie and Miss Emily, they are to attend the wedding, are they not?" asked Sally in a slow, deliberate way.

"Naturally," replied Grandma.

"Seeing as we have no nanny, ma'am, and that I am good with children, maybe I could come to the wedding as a stand-in nanny?"

"How would that be, Penny?" Grandma turned to Penny. Penny nodded while Sally breathed a sigh of relief.

Finally, everyone filed out as Grandma picked up her pen to jot down another note.

"Grandma," Penny watched as Duncan disappeared down the hall. "I don't think Duncan wants to be a butler."

"Whatever do you mean? To be a butler at his age in a house this size is an honour not to mention a substantial raise in pay."

"I know, but I think he wants to build things."

"Ridiculous," Grandma peered at the list in front of her.

"Grandma, why did you give Aunt Colleen and Papa the house?"

Grandma laid down her pen and spoke in a soft, almost whispery, voice. "I could have helped your parents when they married, but I didn't approve of your father. I was stubborn and shall regret my arrogance for the rest of my life. I have the chance to make amends. Your sisters need a mother and that house in Halifax needs a family. We could wait until your father built his house, but Maggie needs a home now. There may be a little talk, the marriage being a rushed sort of affair, but when you have lived as long as I have, you care less about what others think and more about doing what's right. Besides, it is my opinion that your mother would have approved of this union. Who could be better than Colleen to raise Elizabeth's daughters? The war is over. Let's get on with life, shall we?"

Penny wanted to say so much. She wanted to know why it was that no one had asked her how she felt. Must children always be seen but not heard? Instead, she nodded and said nothing, at least nothing really important.

"Could I deliver the invitation to Mrs. O'Malley? I know the way." Penny's eyes watered up although she was hardly aware of it.

"Absolutely n—" Grandma stopped. She looked at Penny and considered. "Perhaps that is a good idea. However, you may not go alone. Arthur has errands to do, but I could spare Duncan for a few hours. Off you go then."

CHAPTER N° 8

Within the hour, Duncan and Penny had caught the streetcar at Atwater, passed the St-Antoine Market, crossed over on the swing bridge, and headed into Verdun.

They climbed off the streetcar at the corner of Galt and Wellington Avenue and carried on down the road.

"Who is it?" Mrs. O'Malley called as the front door opened.

"It's me, Ma, and I've brought a bit of Christmas cheer with me," Duncan hollered as he removed his boots. He pressed his finger to his lips to hush Penny. The two hung up their coats on the hooks by the door.

"Now, Duncan, ya know that I won't have alcohol of any sort in my house," came the merry response.

"With two sons on their way home from the war, Ma, ya might be allowing a pint or two to cross the threshold. But I'm not talking about that kind of cheer at all." Duncan now filled the doorway of the parlour. "Guess what I've brought ya?"

"A fat turkey."

"What I brought is too skinny to make a decent meal," Duncan laughed. Penny peeked around Duncan. Mrs. O'Malley sat in her welcoming buttercup-yellow parlour with a cozy shawl about her shoulders, a bag of wool at her feet, and knitting needles in her hands. A small Christmas tree, not higher than a foot or two, stood on a table. A coal fire was burning in the fireplace.

"Good morning, Mrs. O'Malley. It's me, Penny."

"Is that our Penny? Oh, my dear, it's grand that you are here. And in a few weeks Duncan's two brothers will be home from the war," Mrs. O'Malley said wistfully. "I am one of the lucky ones. But darlin', sit yourself down and tell me how things are with you."

"Right then, ladies, talk on. I've got work to do!" announced Duncan as he shovelled bits of coal on the fire, then went off down the hall, whistling.

"And would you be bringing us a cup then, Duncan?"

"Aye, a man's work is never done," he called from the wee kitchen in the back of the house.

"Now, tell me your news?" smiled Mrs. O'Malley.

"Papa and Aunt Colleen are to be married on Christmas Eve." There, she had said it.

"I see," said Mrs. O'Malley, which was a funny thing to say since Mrs. O'Malley was blind. For a moment neither spoke.

Then the whole story came tumbling out. Penny could not have stopped herself even if she wanted to. They were all to move to Halifax, which was exactly what she had wished for. She didn't feel like a big sister any more. And everyone was making decisions about her life without even talking to her. And, oh, the worst part was— Grandma was *happy*! However it happened, Penny found herself wrapped in Mrs. O'Malley's arms, crying her heart out. "Now, now, my darling girl, in the end it will all turn out right."

Penny sat up and rubbed her face with her sleeve. "Would you come to the wedding? I have the invitation here. Please, oh please, won't you come for me?"

They were late. Penny and Duncan burst through the back door and stomped their feet to shake the snow off. Cook, who spoke through a cloud of flour dust, said that Penny's father was after looking for her. "Along with yea, girl, and don't keep your father waiting. He's in the nursery," scowled Cook.

Penny trudged up the stairs towards Maggie and Emily's bedroom. Papa sat by the window while Maggie and Emily crouched on the floor in front of the dollhouse. The girls were moving furniture around with absolutely no regard for where things belonged. "Emily, you can't put the kitchen table in the drawing room," Penny huffed. "And look where you put the wardrobe!"

"Penny, I am sure you can put it all to rights when they have finished playing. And isn't that why you went to all the work of fixing it up, so that your sisters could play?" said Papa from the far end of the room. Penny nodded. She couldn't help herself. She was just so annoyed.

"I have something for you." Papa motioned to a long, white box on the table.

Penny's heart started to thump in her chest. She knew, she absolutely knew, what was in the box. Slowly she lifted the lid. "Oh, Papa!" It wasn't like the blue dress he had given her just before the explosion. This one was an emerald green velvet dress. Tears welled up in Penny's eyes. It seemed that she had spent the last two days either crying or trying not to cry.

"Your aunt Colleen helped me pick it out. This time all the proper underthings are included," he chuckled.

Penny fingered the lace at the neckline of the dress. "It's the loveliest dress in the world."

"I think your aunt would like to hear that."

"Thank you, Papa." She sniffed and kissed him on the cheek.

Aunt Colleen's door was ajar but Penny knocked softly anyway. "Come in, my dear." Aunt Colleen was sitting at her dressing table.

"Thank you for the dress. It's gorgeous." Aunt Colleen turned and opened her arms. Penny flew cross the room. "It's lovely, really it is. And I am happy that you and Papa are getting married, really I am," she sobbed in Aunt Colleen's arms.

Penny lifted the emerald green velvet dress out of the box.

"It's wonderful that Grandma gave us a house and I love Halifax. And Emily needs a mother more than anyone or else she will always say awful things like piss-pot and numb-bum, but—" Penny hiccupped.

"Penny, did you say yes?" Emily barged into the bedroom.

"Wait, Emily, I haven't asked her yet," Aunt Colleen smiled as she stroked Penny's hair.

"Asked me what?" Penny wiped the tears off her face with the back of her hand.

"I was hoping that you would be my maid of honour," said Aunt Colleen.

"Really?" Penny sniffed again.

"I couldn't think of anyone I would want more."

"I am going to be a bridesmaid, and Maggie is going to be the flower girl." Emily began to dance and twirl in circles. As if on cue, Maggie trundled into the bedroom, leaving Papa to stand on the threshold. "How are my girls?" He looked from Aunt Colleen's face to Penny's, then back again. "Your daughter has just agreed to be my maid of honour," announced Aunt Colleen.

"What does a maid of honour do?" asked Penny.

"She helps the bride. And right now, I need a great deal of help with the flowers, my dress, the shoes. But you were going to tell me something. What was it?" asked Aunt Colleen.

"No, no, it's all right." How could she say what she felt when everyone else was so happy?

"Right, then. Let's go to work."

At that moment, the radiators started to clank. It sounded as if the imaginary animals in the radiators had turned into great whacking monsters having a boxing match.

"It sounds as if Duncan will have his hands full with that furnace again," sighed Aunt Colleen.

"Why don't I give him a hand?" Papa offered. "There is more to being a contractor than just building houses." He went off looking surprisingly jolly about spending the rest of the afternoon tinkering with a temperamental furnace in a cold basement.

"Is the house going to blow up, Penny?" asked Emily.

"Of course not," said Penny. "Papa will fix the furnace and then the house will be fine."

"Papa can fix anything, can't he, Penny?"

"Almost anything," whispered Penny.

CHAPTER Nº 9

December 24, Christmas Eve

Penny dressed alone in her bedroom. She wore a wool chest protector, a soft cotton corset, a straight slip, and then a frilly one. Carefully she stepped into her green velvet dress. It was no mean feat to do the buttons up the back. She looked into the mirror. The girl who peered back looked older and very, very tired. Penny had hardly slept a wink the night before. She had made a decision. She knew what to do, but what would Grandma say? And would Papa ever forgive her?

"It's a regular circus down in the kitchen. Servants for hire indeed!" huffed Sally as she burst into Penny's room. The annoyed look on her face vanished. "Look at yea, sure you're a vision. Come along. Your aunt Colleen needs yea." Sally hustled Penny down the hall.

"Oh, Penny, that emerald green colour on you is perfect, and Sally, you do look lovely too," said Aunt Colleen as the two entered her bedroom. The compliment turned Sally quite pink. For the hundredth time Sally ran her hands down her new, blue wool uniform. She'd be the envy of every nanny in Montreal. Maggie and Emily sat on the floor with their dark ruby-red velvet dresses spread about them. They looked like blond cherubs.

There was a knock at the door. Grandma, as majestic as always, stood in the doorway. She wore an elegant, floor-length silver gown. Her silver hair was swept up in a soft bun, revealing glittering diamond earrings that matched a breathtaking necklace. If Penny was momentarily speechless when seeing Grandma, then Grandma appeared to feel likewise. Her eyes swept across the scene. Colleen turned to face Grandma. Her ivory-coloured satin dress reached mid-calf. Over top, she wore a short cream-coloured cashmere jacket trimmed with white fur. Grandma cleared her throat. "I can see that everyone is ready. You all look acceptable, very acceptable indeed," said Grandma as tears filled her eyes. Penny wanted to rush over and throw her arms around her grandma. *Don't be sad, Grandma.*

"Colleen, I brought you this." Grandma handed Colleen a blue velvet box with the words *Birks* embossed in gold on the lid. Colleen gently opened it.

It was Sally who found her voice first. "Oh, Miss Colleen, a beautiful rope of pearls. You'll wear them, won't you?"

Colleen nodded as she looked up at her aunt. Words seemed to fail her. "Aunt Penelope, you have already ..." Aunt Colleen stuttered.

"I think your own mother would have given

you such a gift on your wedding day," said Grandma. Penny looked away. Sometimes she forgot that Aunt Colleen had also lost her mother and father when she was a girl.

"I hear that Duncan and David had a time of it with that furnace, but it seems to be working better than ever. David tells me that Duncan has agreed to be best man. Obviously, Robert cannot give the bride away and be best man too." If Grandma thought it inappropriate that a butler be the best man at her niece's wedding, she didn't mention it. With her head held high, Grandma left the room and went down to greet the guests.

"Do you know that it is customary for the bride to give a gift to each member of her wedding party?" said Aunt Colleen.

Emily cheered. Aunt Colleen handed one thin blue box to Emily and the other to Maggie. Emily snapped hers open right away but Maggie gave hers to Sally to open.

"Oh, it's pretty," gushed Emily as she dangled a small ruby on a gold chain from her chubby hand.

"Look, Maggie, you have one too. It matches your dress. Come and I'll help you put it on." Sally held an identical necklace up in front of the two-year-old.

"Penny, would you not like to see your necklace?"

She nodded but wished she could shake her head instead. The last thing she wanted was a gift and certainly not one as lovely as a ruby necklace. How was Aunt Colleen going to take Penny's news?

Aunt Colleen slipped the thin box into Penny's hand. She opened it. It wasn't a ruby. It was an emerald set in gold. "See how it matches your eyes?" Oh, this wasn't fair. Aunt Colleen was making everything so much more difficult.

One of the hired servants poked her head around the door. "Ma'am, I've been sent to tell you that the guests have all arrived."

Aunt Colleen pinned on a small white hat, lowered a short veil over her eyes, and stood.

Penny, Emily, even Maggie, were transfixed. Their new mother was a stunning bride.

"Your flowers." Penny handed Aunt Colleen a bouquet of baby's breath, heather, and deep red roses. As she assumed her duties as maid of honour, Penny could feel the emerald burning on her neck. How could she take such a gift knowing that she was about to cause—what? Damage, harm, hurt? It was agony not knowing what would happen or what to do.

"Come, girls." Sally handed each girl a small bouquet, then took hold of Maggie's hand.

Penny followed her sisters, and Sally too since Maggie was too little to walk down the stairs alone. Uncle Robert stood at the bottom of the staircase, beaming. With dozens of candles lighting their way, the wedding party walked slowly through the main foyer towards the drawing room. The pianist and harpist played softly in the distance, making the great house seem hushed and church-like. Sally let go of Maggie's hand and the two little girls stepped into the drawing room. Penny followed. What she saw nearly took her breath away! The Christmas tree was lit by hundreds of candles. The light shimmered and danced in the mirrors, making it seem as if a million candles illuminated the room.

All the guests stood as the wedding party entered. Gwen was there alongside her mother. She hadn't seen Gwen since they had gone skating together. Imagine what she must be thinking. One minute she says that Papa and Aunt Colleen are sweet on each other and the next she receives an invitation to their wedding! Mrs. Meighen was there and so was Mrs. O'Malley. Oh, how lovely she looked in her best dress. Dr. Finn stood next to her. He may have been a bit confused about receiving an invitation to Aunt Colleen and Papa's wedding, but he looked as if he was enjoying himself enormously. Aunt Colleen's friends were scattered among the guests.

At the top of the room, to one side of the bespectacled Reverend Munsen, Penny saw Papa.

*Penny handed Aunt Colleen a
bouquet of baby's breath,
heather, and deep red roses.*

He looked handsome and happier than she had seen him in a very long time. Duncan, in a new suit and looking very much the gentlemen, stood beside him. Penny smiled at Papa, but he didn't notice. He wasn't looking at her. He was looking past her at Aunt Colleen, his bride. The ceremony began. In a swirl of words, they became a family. Penny almost cried.

CHAPTER Nº 10

"Speech, speech!" someone cried. *Uncle* Robert stood in front of the Christmas tree, held his champagne glass aloft, and said that he had had the good fortune to serve with many a brave soldier from the Royal Ulster Regiment in France. It was from these brave lads that he'd learned these words, "To my beautiful sister and my new brother-in-law: May peace and plenty be the first to lift the latch on your door, and happiness be guided to your home by the candle of Christmas. *Nollaig faoi shéan is faoi shonas daoibh.* A prosperous and happy Christmas to you."

"Nollaig shonas daoibh!" Papa and Aunt Colleen repeated in Irish to all. Happy Christmas!

"Is it not lovely to hear the Irish," said Mrs. O'Malley. Penny agreed, although her thoughts were not on the toast.

"I can't tell you how delighted I am to make the acquaintance of this wonderful woman," beamed Dr. Finn. Mrs. O'Malley blushed. Duncan, standing to one side of his mother, rolled his eyes.

"Dinner is served," announced the for-hire butler. Guests joined their dinner partners and stood outside the closed doors to the dining room. With a flourish, the for-hire butler cast open the dining room doors. Grandma and Uncle Robert led the procession into the room, followed by Papa and ... Aunt Colleen. What would Penny call her now?

"If your son would permit me, would you do me the honour of being my dinner companion this evening?" Dr. Finn bowed to Mrs. O'Malley.

"Nothing would give me more pleasure. I am sure my son can fend for himself," smiled

Mrs. O'Malley as she extended her arm. Dr. Finn took it and placed her hand, ever so gently, on his own outstretched arm.

"Did ya ever see the like? That fellow is as bold as brass! 'Twas me who brought her and look at me now. Left on me own! Do I have you to thank for introducing my dear mother to that old codger?" Duncan turned to Penny. His eyebrows were so high up on his forehead that they reached his hairline. For the first time in days Penny almost laughed. "Well, yea might as well take my arm, for sure it appears that the only way to get fed is to pretend that we're all loading onto the Ark, two by two." Penny took Duncan's arm and they followed Gwen and her mother into the dining room.

Maggie and Emily, both perched on cushions, sat beside Sally at the long table. Between the courses, anxiety rose up in Penny then subsided again. She would have to tell them and soon. If she only knew how to say what she wanted to say!

The grandfather clock announced midnight. It was Christmas Day. The guests had left, Maggie and Emily had been put to bed, and now, in the Irish tradition, the family was having a midnight supper of tea and sandwiches. While everyone gathered around the fire sipping tea, Penny sat alone in the window seat and looked out into the Christmas night. This would be a good time for a miracle, a sign, something to tell her that she was about to do the right thing.

"Aunt Penelope, why don't we give Penny one of her Christmas presents now? That one in the square box," said Aunt Colleen.

"Very well," said Grandma.

Penny's stomach was in knots. She didn't want any gifts. Papa brought the box over to her and sat beside her. The lid came off easily, and there it was ... a small copy of the portrait of Mama that hung in Grandma's room. "Your aunt Colleen arranged this some time ago," he said.

For the first time in two days, Penny didn't want to cry. Instead, she held Mama's portrait close. "I never told anyone, but after the explosion, Maggie and Emily were trapped under the pram. A piece of wood fell over it and I couldn't budge it. A lady came along and lifted it off for me. I thought that it was too heavy for a *mortal* person, and she knew that my gloves were in my pocket, and ..." Papa didn't speak for a moment as if taking time to put it all together.

"And you thought Mama had come back to help. Oh, my dear." He put his arms around his daughter and the two rocked back and forth. "She is with us, darlin' girl, but in spirit."

"I know, Papa, and I know that you and, and ..." Penny stumbled. What should she call Aunt Colleen? "I know that you will both be happy. I am glad that you are married and that Maggie will have *permanence.*"

Papa paused then looked towards the servants' door. "So you overheard my conversation with your grandmother?"

"I'm sorry. I know it was wrong to listen, but I have to tell you something."

"Tell me what, my girl?"

"I can't come with you to Halifax."

No one across the room suspected a thing. Penny spoke in a whisper and Papa just listened. He did not interrupt or ask any questions. It felt good to be listened to. But Papa did not like what he heard. His forehead crinkled and his lips were pulled so tight they were nothing but a thin line. Penny stopped talking and waited. She should have felt anxious, but oddly she felt calmer than she had in days! Finally, Papa took her hand and the two walked over to the fireplace.

"We have an announcement to make. And for the record—" Papa looked towards his new wife "—I approve."

"What is it? Don't keep us in suspense." Grandma disliked surprises at any time of the year.

"I am not going to move to Halifax, Grandma. I want to stay with you."

The room grew very quiet. Grandma did not speak for a bit, and when she did, her voice warbled.

"My darling girl, that means the world to me, but I cannot allow it. You must go with your family."

"But you don't understand, Grandma. I *am* with my family. Gwen once said that I had two families, but I don't have two families. I have one family in two places. I will stay in Montreal for the school year and in the summers we can both go back to Halifax. Grandma, it's what I want. I love you."

Grandma's hands shook and her teacup might have fallen to the floor had Penny not been there to catch it.

CHAPTER N° 11

January 2, 1919

"Remember, deportment is the hallmark of refinement. There is no need to be overly demonstrative. Simply wave goodbye in a lady-like fashion." Everyone, Penny, Grandma, Aunt Colleen, Papa, Emily, Maggie, Duncan, and even Arthur, passed under the steel-arched glass roof of Windsor Station and trooped across the station to the train platform.

"Yes, Grandma," smiled Penny as she passed Grandma an extra hanky. Great billows of smoke poured from the train's smokestack as it made ready to leave.

"You take care of yourself." Sally threw her arms around Penny.

"And you," said Penny. "I'm glad you are going with Maggie and Emily, really I am." Sally would make a good nanny.

"Wait!" Despite his limp, Uncle Robert strode across the train station. Over the past few days, he had regained his colour. Although he was still occasionally out of breath, he had come a long way. "Here are some candies for the girls, a magazine for my darling sister, and a Montreal *Gazette* for my new brother-in-law."

Colleen laughed then put her arms around Penny. "Go on. Give it a try."

"Colleen," giggled Penny.

"Again."

"Colleen." This time Penny laughed out loud. Calling Aunt Colleen *Colleen* would take some getting used to.

"Good girl. It seems silly calling me Mama. It's

different for the girls." Penny nodded and hugged Colleen yet again.

A whistle blew again. "It's time," said Papa.

Duncan swept Sally up in his arms and planted a smacking big kiss on her mouth right in front of everyone. "We'll be together soon," he said. Sally's face turned tomato red but she giggled just the same.

"You have an apprenticeship waiting for you when you are ready to take it on. You'll make a fine master builder one day." Papa held out his hand to Duncan, and the two men gave each other firm handshakes.

"Thank you, sir. I cannot leave my mother until my brothers are home from the war and Mrs. Underhill has employed a new butler, but I hope to be in Halifax by spring."

"Here, Emily, this is for you." Penny reached into the bag and pulled out Martha. "Take good care of her." Emily squealed in delight as she gave the doll a hug. "Goodbye, Maggie. I will love you forever and ever. And remember,

Grandma will ship all Mama's toys to the new house."

Penny again threw her arms around her little sister. With her thumb plugged into her mouth and one hand curling a wisp of hair, Maggie nodded. Maggie would speak when she was ready. They would all just have to be patient.

"You are very sure about this?" Papa asked Penny.

"I am, Papa. Very sure."

"You are your mother's daughter, my darlin' girl." Papa swung Maggie up into his arms and in a flurry of waves, they were gone.

"See you in the summer," Penny called after them. A flood of people rushed past, compartment doors slammed shut, and the train lurched out of the station. Suddenly it was very quiet.

"I think this calls for lunch at the Ritz Carlton," announced Uncle Robert.

"Right you are, sir," said Arthur. "I shall drop you three off then run Duncan home."

"You misunderstand me, Arthur, we shall *all* go to lunch at The Ritz. Times are changing. The day may come when it is acceptable for servants and gentry to have lunch together."

"Oh, I hope not. I shouldn't like that at all, sir."

"Oh, for goodness' sake, you old buffalo, just say yes," snapped Grandma.

"Since you put it so eloquently ma'am, Duncan and I accept your invitation."

Duncan grinned at Penny. Knowing that a new life awaited him in Halifax had made his present position something to be appreciated.

"The Ritz it is. Come, Penny." Grandma took Penny's arm and grandmother and granddaughter walked across the great expanse of the station. "Do you know that when I was your age, I toured Europe? I was on *La Grand Tour*. Of course, Europe is in a bit of a mess at the moment, and there is this influenza to consider, but this will pass."

"Are we going to travel, Grandma?"

"With your father's permission, of course. You must see Rome and London, of course, Madrid naturally. And no rounded education would be complete without visiting Paris. Although I myself would like to visit the pyramids ..."

Uncle Robert laughed as he put his arm around Penny. "It seems that the adventure has just begun."

Acknowledgements

My thanks to:

Ian (David) McKay, careful reader

Barbara Berson, editor

Dawn Hunter, copy editor

Cathy MacLean, designer

Catherine Dorton, production editor

Denise Verge, the cover model for penny

Mary Donahoe, the model for Aunt Colleen

Dear Reader,

This has been the fourth and final book about Penny. We hope you've enjoyed meeting and getting to know her as much as we have enjoyed bringing her—and her wonderful story—to you.

Although Penny's tale is told, there are still eleven more terrific girls to read about, whose exciting adventures take place in Canada's past—girls just like you. So do keep on reading!

And please—don't forget to keep in touch! We love receiving your incredible letters telling us about your favourite stories and which girls you like best. And thank you for telling us about the stories you would like to read! There are so many remarkable stories in Canadian history. It seems that wherever we live, great stories live too, in our towns and cities, on our rivers and mountains. We hope that Our Canadian Girl *captures the richness of that past.*

Sincerely,
    Barbara Berson

Canada's

1608
Samuel de Champlain establishes the first fortified trading post at Quebec.

1759
The British defeat the French in the Battle of the Plains of Abraham.

1812
The United States declares war against Canada.

1845
The expedition of Sir John Franklin to the Arctic ends when the ship is frozen in the pack ice; the fate of its crew remains a mystery.

1869
Louis Riel leads his Métis followers in the Red River Rebellion.

1871
British Columbia joins Canada.

1755
The British expel the entire French population of Acadia (today's Maritime provinces), sending them into exile.

1776
The 13 Colonies revolt against Britain, and the Loyalists flee to Canada.

1837
Calling for responsible government, the Patriotes, following Louis-Joseph Papineau, rebel in Lower Canada; William Lyon Mackenzie leads the uprising in Upper Canada.

1867
New Brunswick, Nova Scotia, and the United Province of Canada come together in Confederation to form the Dominion of Canada.

1870
Manitoba joins Canada. The Northwest Territories become an official territory of Canada.

1762
Elizabeth

Timeline

1885
At Craigellachie, British Columbia, the last spike is driven to complete the building of the Canadian Pacific Railway.

1898
The Yukon Territory becomes an official territory of Canada.

1914
Britain declares war on Germany, and Canada, because of its ties to Britain, is at war too.

1918
As a result of the Wartime Elections Act, the women of Canada are given the right to vote in federal elections.

1945
World War II ends conclusively with the dropping of atomic bombs on Hiroshima and Nagasaki.

1873
Prince Edward Island joins Canada.

1896
Gold is discovered on Bonanza Creek, a tributary of the Klondike River.

1905
Alberta and Saskatchewan join Canada.

1917
In the Halifax harbour, two ships collide, causing an explosion that leaves more than 1,600 dead and 9,000 injured.

1939
Canada declares war on Germany seven days after war is declared by Britain and France.

1949
Newfoundland, under the leadership of Joey Smallwood, joins Canada.

1885
Marie-Claire

1897
Emily

1939
Ellen